The Big Adventures of Little Prince Anton

By
Sue York

AuthorHouse™ UK
1663 Liberty Drive
Bloomington, IN 47403 USA
www.authorhouse.co.uk
Phone: 0800 047 8203 (Domestic TFN)
+44 1908 723714 (International)

ISBN: 978-1-7283-9302-5 (sc)
ISBN: 978-1-7283-9303-2 (e)

Print information available on the last page.

Published by AuthorHouse 10/08/2019

authorHOUSE®

This book is dedicated to my wonderful family
for all their encouragement.

A special thank you to George for supplying me with
constant cups of tea.

Hello everyone, I would like to share with you a little story about something that happened one day to a tiny creature who lived near my home.

It all began one hot Summer day in a small Bluebell wood at the bottom of my Mum's garden. Although the Bluebells have now gone until next Spring, there are many wildflowers scattered all through the wood.

Fluttering over these flowers, looking like coloured paper shapes on strands of thin elastic thread, are lots of different coloured butterflies. From a tiny Blue, with wings only as wide as half my little finger, to the largest, and very rare Swallowtail butterfly. Of all the butterflies there, I think these are my favourite. What do you think?

There is also a small pond in the wood. It doesn't have any fish in it, but in the Spring you can see hundreds of Tadpoles swimming around through the pond weeds, like tiny black balloons with wriggly tails. But now it is Summer, they have all grown into beautiful frogs.

Flying over the pond in the Summer sun are yellow, blue, green and red dragonflies hunting for big juicy flies to eat.

Up in all the trees you can see and hear lots of different birds. Pink jays squawk and bounce from branch to branch. They make a sound just like someone brushing up crispy leaves.

Bright green woodpeckers, hammer the bark of the trees with their beaks, looking for grubs to eat. They are answered in the distance by black and white woodpeckers with a bright red spot on their heads.

This is a beautiful spot any time of year and I come here to sit and draw, or paint. This is where I had my ideas and painted some of the pictures you are looking at in this book.

Sometimes I take photographs and sometimes I just sit and listen to the sounds of the creatures who live in this magical place. Here are a few of my photographs and paintings.

In one corner of this tiny wood, is a giant old Oak tree.

Grey squirrels chase each other round and round the huge tree trunk, chattering as they try to catch up with their playmate.

The tree has many large twisting roots which make little hiding places for different animals. When my Granddaughters were little, they would pretend they were playing hide and seek with the fairies, among the roots of this old tree.

But that will be another story for me to tell you sometime.

Today, my story is about an ant Prince called Anton and the adventures and misadventures he had when he left his colony (that is what a nest of ants is called) and went off in search of his young Queen.

Come with me, as we go back to the day this little ant had some very big adventures.

My story begins, deep inside the roots of the old giant Oak tree. A huge ant nest has been built there and this is where our little friend Anton hatched, along with hundreds of brothers and sisters. He wasn't born like us, because ants lay eggs. His mother, the Queen, lays thousands of eggs which are taken to a nursery chamber to be cared for by the youngest workers.

The other worker ants are the oldest females of the colony (except for the Queen) and work very hard gathering food and protecting the nest.

Anton is part of a huge family of Princes, young Queens and workers. The nest is enormous and has lots of tunnels and rooms.

Some are food storerooms, and some are nurseries. This is where all the eggs are kept and where Anton and his brothers and sisters are cared for by Nanny and her helpers until they hatch. The Queen lays eggs, which change into tiny white grubs. The workers feed and clean the grubs until they change into soft white silky cocoons. After a while the young ant inside breaks out of the protective shell.

Here he is, just hatched from his cocoon and fully grown.

Anton and his brothers and sisters have wings. They are Princes and young Queens. Only the royal members of the colony have wings. Their job is to fly away and make new nests.

But Anton wants to stay behind to help Nanny look after the new eggs the Queen has laid. Nanny is the oldest worker in the whole colony and everyone, including the Queen, loves her.

He tries to stretch out his wings, but they are still wet and crumpled after being in the cocoon. He was the last to hatch and is the last one left in the nursery and is soon joined by Nanny.

"There you are! So, this is where you have been hiding!" said Nanny, who is a little bit out of breath. "I've been looking everywhere for you. All your brothers and sisters have already flown away .... come along .... stop fidgeting with your wings it's time to go." She tries to push him out with her broom. "But Nanny," replies Anton, "my wings are not dry yet." Nanny looks over the top of her glasses at him. "If you go outside into the warm sun, they will soon dry. Go on .....off you go ..... I have a lot of work to do. The nursery has to be cleaned ready for the new eggs." She pushes him again with her broom.

"I can help you," said Anton, "I am strong you know, I can do lots of jobs for you and I can help you look after the new eggs." Nanny is shocked at Anton suggesting such a thing. "You will do nothing of the kind! What would

11

your mother say if she knew I was letting a Prince do my work?" She starts brushing the floor. "Thank you, Anton, you are very kind, but you have an important job to do. As a Prince, you must find a Queen and start a new colony." Reluctantly, Anton hugs Nanny then walks through the doorway, down the tunnel and out of sight.

There is a tear in Nanny's eye as she watches him go.

Anton walks out of the tunnel into the sunshine, but the light is so bright it makes his eyes hurt.

He walks very carefully but does not know that he is walking along a very tall thin flower stem. He does not know he is in danger! The sunlight is so bright, he still cannot see clearly. Suddenly a gust of wind throws him off balance. He loses his grip and falls...down...down and down...until...plop! Something has stopped his fall.

As he tries to turn around to climb down from the soft net he has fallen into, he realises he cannot move, he is stuck...like glue! The more he wriggles, the stronger he is stuck, until his body, every leg, his head and his wings are all stuck fast.

"Oh great, now I can't move at all!" He struggles again to get free but with no luck.

As he lies there thinking how he can get himself free, he does not know he is being watched. He does not know that he has fallen into a spider's web, and he does not know that the spider, who built the web, is creeping very slowly towards him. The spider has a big grin on his face.

As Anton's eyes eventually get used to the sunlight, he sees the trouble he is in. As he looks around, he sees the spider, with his two sharp teeth, slowly creeping up to him. He does not realise that spiders like to eat ants as well as other things that fly into and get caught up in their sticky webs. Remember I told you that Anton is of royal blood, so he has been taught good manners. He greets the spider as best he can, but the spider does not reply. "Excuse me," Anton calls again, "could you please be so kind as to help me, I seem to be very stuck."

The spider stops, grins the biggest grin you could ever imagine, then quickly grabs poor Anton by his wings.

Now, if you are too frightened, I could leave my story here, but if I did you would never know what happened next.

So, the spider tries to pull Anton away from the web, but he has become too tangled up with the sticky silk. Spiders spin their webs from a special silk which is made in their bodies. It is very sticky and also very strong.

The spider looks at Anton and speaks to him with a kind, soft voice. "Well young lad, you have got yourself into a pickle. Don't you worry I'll soon have you free."

Well now...I bet you didn't expect that did you?

The spider quickly cuts Anton free from the web. "There you are youngster, let me help you down. I'm Sammy and I'm very sorry you got caught in my web. I spin them to catch flies but spend most of my time cutting free the bees. I don't like catching them because bees make honey which is very good for human children."

Sammy looks back at what is left of his web. "Oh dear," he said, "it looks like I am going to have to make another one. Never mind, at least you are safe."

Sammy carries Anton over to a mushroom and puts him down to rest.

Lilly the ladybird is sitting nearby and sees how tired and weak Anton is and she tells Sammy that she will go and ask her friend Beatrix the bumble bee for help. She knows that eating some sweet honey will soon make Anton feel better. Lilly flies off to find her friend Beatrix. She spots her on her favourite flowers, the Poppies.

After telling her all about what has happened to poor Anton, they both fly off to ask the honeybees for help. The honeybees are good friends of Beatrix and they agree to give her some of their lovely honey. They put the golden honey into some small Foxglove flowers.

This makes it easier for Beatrix to pack into the baskets on her legs. When the baskets are full, she and Lilly both fly off to find Sammy and Anton.

When they arrive, Beatrix gives Anton some sips of the honey. He dips his tongue into the Foxglove flower and drinks the deliciously sweet, golden honey.

All ants love anything sweet. He starts to feel stronger in a few minutes and he thanks Beatrix very much for getting the honey for him.

"So how did you get yourself into so much trouble?" asked Beatrix. "I was on my way to find my Queen," he explained, "when a gust of wind blew me into Sammy's web. Can you please help me because I think I am lost?"

Beatrix tells him that she has seen a swarm of flying ants going across the meadow. Lilly immediately corrects Beatrix and tell her that a group of flying ants is called a cloud. They argue who is right until Sammy tells them they are both right. A group of flying ants can be called either a cloud or a swarm. They all laugh about how silly it was to argue about a name and then Beatrix tells Anton that when he is feeling better and strong enough to fly, she will show him where she saw the other flying ants.

After eating the honey and resting a while in the warm sunshine, Anton's wings are dry and are now strong enough for him to fly.

Remember I told you what a very polite young ant he is, so he says goodbye to Sammy and thanks him for cutting him free from the web and for not eating him. Beatrix and Lilly laugh because they know how many times Sammy has to mend or rebuild his web every day, whenever a bee gets caught in it.

Beatrix tells Anton she will show him the way to the meadow so he can look for all the other ants and the three of them, Beatrix, Lilly and Anton, wave goodbye to Sammy and fly off together.

They had only been flying a few minutes when suddenly they hear chattering laughter behind them. It is getting louder and louder. Then, they hear a high screech and scream and a whoosh of wind as a huge white bird swoops down over the top of our three friends. It is Sean the seagull and he is in a very bad mood. In fact, Sean is always in a very bad mood but today he has a sore wing, so he is in a worse mood than ever.

"Ha, ha, ha, ha, ha, I am going to have a big juicy bee for my lunch," he squawks, "followed by a ladybird and ant desert." He chases them but because his wing is sore, he cannot fly as fast as they can.

Bit by bit he is getting closer. His huge beak wide open ready to eat our three little friends. Beatrix knows just how mean and bad-tempered Sean is and tells Lilly and Anton to quickly find somewhere to hide, while she distracts him.

Lilly sees some litter someone has left on the grass below. There is a long straw which she thinks looks just big enough for them to crawl into. "Anton, follow me, I think we can hide in that straw, we should be safe there, his beak is too big to get inside."

Beatrix does a great job distracting Sean. She flies just slow enough for him to think he can catch her, then as he gets close, she swoops down into a patch of wildflowers, through the stems and back out the other side of the bushes.

Sean cannot see her anywhere. She sees a little mouse hole and flies down and hides inside.

Just then the mouse comes back home, very out of breath. She has seen Sean and knows that he would eat her if he could. She runs inside her mouse hole and bumps right into Beatrix. "Oh no," she squeaks, "who are you, and why are you in my home? Are you going to eat me?"

Molly, that is this little mouse's name, is a very nervous mouse. She has been like this ever since she was separated from the rest of her family, when the field they were living in flooded in a storm.

Beatrix tries to comfort poor Molly and tells her she will not harm her. She asks if she can hide in her home for a little while until Sean flies away. Molly agrees, she too is frightened of Sean, but then poor Molly is frightened of everything.

At the same time all this is happening, Anton and Lilly quickly fly down and run into the straw. Sean can't find Beatrix, so he flies back to where he last saw his ant and ladybird meal. He glides round and round above the pile of litter, trying to find them.

When I see seagulls flying around like this, it reminds me of watching people flying their kites up high in the air, silently twisting, turning and diving.

When I was a child, I loved to fly my kite. I wasn't very good at it, and it often got caught up in the tree branches in the park. If you have a kite and like to fly it, the best time is on a windy day and the best place is away from trees. Go to a big patch of grass in the park or if you lived near a beach you could go there. But remember to stay away from the water.

Now, to get back to my story.

Sean lands in the middle of all the litter. He picks up bits and pieces in his beak to see if Lilly and Anton are hiding under anything. Our little friends can hear him getting closer and closer. Then….suddenly Sean grabs the straw in his beak. Anton and Lilly hold on as tight as they can, as Sean runs across the grass, flaps his wings and flies off with them.

Lilly whispers to Anton to stay quiet and hold on tight. She knows they will be safe as long as they can stay in the straw. Sean flies across the meadow to the top of a tall building where he is helping his wife to build a nest. Seagulls usually do not make neat shaped nests like some other birds. They just gather together some stones, twigs and anything else they like the look of, like the straw which our friends are hiding inside.

Beatrix looks outside Molly's mouse hole to see if she can see Sean. He is nowhere in sight. She takes the last honey filled foxglove flower out of her basket and gives it to Molly, and thanks her for letting her stay. Molly smells the honey and smiles. It reminds her when her brothers and sisters were given a piece of honeycomb her parents had found.

She sticks her nose deep into the flower and licks up some of the honey. When she lifts out her head, her nose and whiskers are covered in the sticky golden honey.

She licks her mouth and wipes off the honey with her paws.

Then, she sits down and slowly licks her paws clean. She was so busy with the honey, she had not noticed that Beatrix had flown away.

Beatrix flies back to where she told her two friends to hide. Bees are very good remembering directions. She sees how Sean had scattered the litter all over the grass, and panics, thinking her friends have been caught. "Ooooh, I think that seagull is so mean," she buzzes, "I think he has to be taught a lesson in manners."

She flies off looking for any sign of where Sean has gone. In the distance she hears him screeching and laughing. Beatrix thinks he is laughing because of what he has done.

"I know what will stop him laughing." She says and flies off to find Sammy. She knows that although other seagulls would happily eat a spider, there is one seagull who is frightened of them and his name is Sean.

Beatrix finds Sammy sitting in the middle of his nice new web. He has been busy all morning making a new one. "Hello my dear," he says, when he sees Beatrix, "have you been able to find Anton's brothers and sisters already? That was quick." He sees how upset Beatrix looks. "Why, what is the matter my dear, you look so worried."

Beatrix sits on a leaf at the side of Sammy's web and tells him the awful trouble they have been in, how they were chased and how they had to hide from that horrible, bad tempered Sean. She tells him that she can hear him laughing from across the meadow and she fears that something horrible has happened to Anton and Lilly.

"He is such a bully, and I think you are the only thing that frightens him. Will you come with me to teach him a lesson, not to be so mean?" she asks Sammy. "Of course I will my dear. I just hope you are wrong and the two of them are hiding from Sean."

Beatrix tells Sammy to climb on her back and she will fly them to where she heard the laughing. Now, although bumble bees are very strong, they would not normally be strong enough to carry a spider as big as Sammy. But Beatrix is so angry with Sean it has given her the extra strength she needs.

They find Sean sitting on the rooftop, squawking and chattering to himself. He doesn't see them creeping up to him until it is too late. The shock of seeing Sammy makes him fall off the roof but just in time he spreads out his wings and flies away.

Anton and Lilly have been safely hiding in the straw and when they hear Sammy and Beatrix laughing at Sean they crawl out. They are all so happy to see each other again and there are big hugs all round. "I thought something awful had happened to you both," said Beatrix as she hugged them. "I am so happy to see you are safe."

Just then they hear someone or something squeaking. They look down and on the ground is a little brown mouse, calling to them. Beatrix flies down to see what she wants.

When she sees the little mouse, she thinks it is Molly. "Hello again Molly, how did you find us?" The little mouse looked very puzzled. "My name is Millie not Molly," she replied, "I had a sister called Molly, but we were separated when our home flooded."

Beatrix cannot believe what she hears. "I know your sister," she said, "she helped me hide from Sean the seagull." Millie shook with fear at that name. She knew all about Sean. Her Mother had told her to run and hide if she ever saw or heard any seagulls, especially Sean. "Did you say you know my sister Molly?" She asked Beatrix. "Where is she? Is she here with you now?" She looked up to where Beatrix had been. "No, she is not here but I can take you to where she lives."

The little mouse had tears of happiness rolling down her cheeks. "Oh yes please," she squeaked, "I would love to see my sister again."

Lilly and Anton fly down to Beatrix and Millie. As Sammy cannot fly, he uses his silk, sticking it to the roof and gliding down to the ground. Beatrix tells them all about how a little mouse called Molly had helped her hide from Sean. She tells them that Molly had lost her family when their home was flooded. She introduces Millie to everyone and tells them that she is Molly's missing sister. She says that she is going to take Millie to Molly's home just as soon as she has taken Sammy back to his web. Millie tells Sammy that he can ride on her back as she is much stronger than Beatrix.

Anton looks very unhappy when he hears that Beatrix will not be able to show him where she saw the other ants. He thinks that by the time she comes back, it will be too late, and they will have all flown away. But Beatrix had other plans. She tells Lilly exactly where she saw the other ants and tells Anton that Lilly can take him there.

Everyone is happy. They all say their goodbyes. Sammy is going to get a ride home, Millie is going to find her sister again and Lilly is taking Anton to find his Queen. A happy ending for everyone, except Sean. He has nightmares about Sammy for a whole week. Serves him right for being so mean.

I hope you have liked my story about Anton and his new friends. I look forward to telling you my next one very soon.

Printed in the United States
By Bookmasters